Bebé Goes Shopping

Susan Middleton Elya

Illustrated by
Steven Salerno

Harcourt, Inc.

Orlando   Austin   New York   San Diego   Toronto   London

Manufactured in China

A day at the market,
a really big store—

the **supermercado**—
with groceries galore.

Bebé in the shopping cart, high in the seat,
looks all around for a **dulce**—a sweet.

Mamá wears a dress—a **vestido bonito**.
It blocks **Bebé's** view as she steers the **carrito**.

But then she bends down to a near-the-floor shelf.
Mamá's disappeared!

Time to reach things himself.

He tugs on a carton with **much**os **colores**
in butterfly yellow, with pink and white **flores**.

Mamá sees him holding it, gives him a kiss.
"Why, sweetie," she murmurs,
"that's here on my list."

The next aisle over, **Mamá** finds the rice.

Bebé squeals and kicks her.

"**Querido**, be nice!"

Mamá steps away, but she doesn't go far.
Bebé helps himself to a good-looking jar.
"**Ay, hijo,**" she says, "keep your hands to yourself."
She dives for the jar, puts it back on the shelf.

Bebé picks out corn as **Mamá** chooses peas.
She grabs the **maíz** as she takes out her keys.

"Just play with my **llaves**," she says.
"**¡Por favor!**"
He giggles and drops them.

They clank on the floor.

Bebé leans and reaches. **Mamá** has to shout.
"**¡Cuidado!**" she warns him, so he won't fall out.

Mamá keeps on shopping, her list in his sight.
Bebé chews the corner, just one little bite.

She throws up her **manos**, then snatches the list
(except for the part he holds tight in his fist).

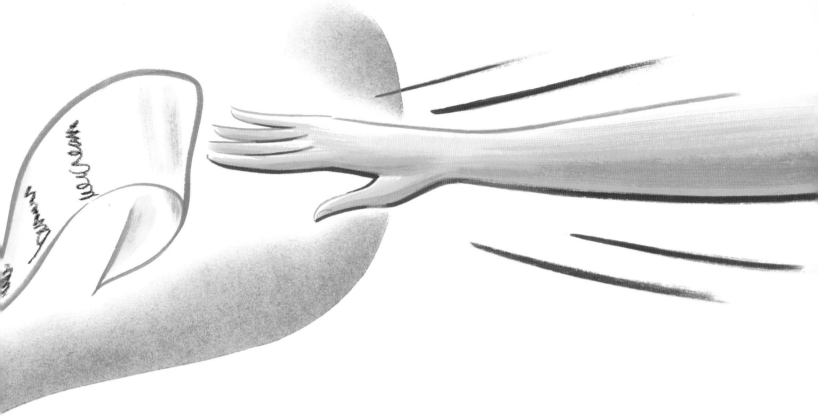

A nosy **señora** comes up. "Cootchie-coo!
It's hard to be good when there's nothing to do."

Mamá rolls her eyes, sees a circus display.
"**Est**o," she says, "is your snack for the day."

Bebé shakes the **caja**, hears cookies inside.
But it doesn't open. He's tried and he's tried.

She pulls back the box top. . . .

He grabs a **león**.

RRRRRI

Mamá heads to Produce to choose a **melón**.

Bebé finds a camel—a humpy **sorpresa**!

Mamá picks a good one. He eats the **cabeza**.

While she shops for **queso**, he finds a giraffe.

In Dairy, **Bebé** bites
the long neck in half.

Mamá checks her watch as **Bebé** eats an oso,

GRR

RRRR

so grumbly and growly
—so **delicioso!**

They empty the cart for the cheery **cajero**,

who rings up their items
and takes the **diner**o.

The manager gives out balloons. They are free.
"**Un**o for your baby?"

Mamá answers, "**Sí.**"

Then comes a final choice:
"Paper or **plástico**?"

Sweet **Bebé** giggles.

His day's been **fantástic**o.

Smiles from **Mamá**.
"Shopping's done! **¡Terminé!**"
And who's been her wonderful helper?

¡Bebé!

Glossary

ay, hijo (I, EE-hoe): oh, son

bebé (beh-BEH): baby

cabeza (kah-BEH-sah): head

caja (KAH-hah): box

cajero (kah-HEH-roe): cashier

carrito (kah-RREE-toe): shopping cart

cuidado (kwee-DAH-doe): careful

delicioso (deh-lee-SYOE-soe): delicious

dinero (dee-NEH-roe): money

dulce (DOOL-seh): sweet

esto (EHS-toe): this

fantástico (fahn-TAHS-tee-koe): fantastic

flores (FLOE-rehs): flowers

llaves (YAH-vehs): keys

león (leh-OWN): lion

maíz (mah-EECE): corn

mamá (mah-MAH): mom

manos (MAH-noce): hands

melón (meh-LOWN): cantaloupe

muchos colores (MOO-choce koe-LOE-rehs): many colors

oso (OE-soe): bear

plástico (PLAHS-tee-koe): plastic

por favor (POHR fah-VOHR): please

querido (keh-REE-doe): sweetie, dear

queso (KEH-soe): cheese

señora (seh-NYOE-rah): woman

sí (SEE): yes

sorpresa (sohr-PREH-sah): surprise

supermercado (soo-pehr-mehr-KAH-doe): supermarket

terminé (tehr-mee-NEH): I finished

uno (OO-noe): one

vestido bonito (vehs-TEE-doe boe-NEE-toe): pretty dress

To Alanna, Candy, Courtney, Elizabeth, Haley, Janine, Jessica, Krista,
Lauren, Leslie, Mackenzie, Mary Kate, Rachel, Sammie, and Syena
—S. M. E.

To Margery Cuyler, thank you for your support and guidance from the beginning
—S. S.

www.HarcourtBooks.com

Library of Congress Cataloging-in-Publication Data
Elya, Susan Middleton, 1955–
Baby goes shopping/Susan Middleton Elya; illustrated by Steven Salerno.
p.   cm.
Summary: Rhyming text describes a trip to the grocery store for a mamá and her baby boy. Includes Spanish words.
[1. Babies—Fiction.   2. Grocery shopping—Fiction.   3. Supermarkets—Fiction.
4. Spanish language—Vocabulary.   5. Stories in rhyme.]
I. Salerno, Steven, ill.   II. Title.
PZ8.3.E514Bab   2006
[E]—dc22   2004022787
ISBN-13: 978-0152-05426-7   ISBN-10: 0-15-205426-X

First edition
A C E G H F D B

The illustrations in this book were created using gouache, watercolors, colored inks,
and colored pencils on French Arches 260 lb hot pressed watercolor paper.
The display type was set in GillSans.
The text type was set in Collins.
Color separations by Bright Arts Ltd., Hong Kong
Manufactured by South China Printing Company, Ltd., China
This book was printed on totally chlorine-free Stora Enso Matte paper.
Production supervision by Pascha Gerlinger
Designed by April Ward